By Sydney Malone

ISBN 978-1-338-13556-5

10 9 8 7 6 5 4 3 2 1 17 18 19 20 21

Printed in the U.S.A. 132

First printing 2017

Book design by Erin McMahon

SCHOLASTIC INC.

Apple Blossom is running for mayor of Shopville! Lippy Lips and Cheeky Chocolate are helping her film a campaign video.

Suzie Sundae comes by to invite them to the park. "Do you even have to campaign? You are, like, totally going to win," Suzie says. "Who else is even running?"

But Apple Blossom isn't the only candidate. Kooky Cookie is running, too.

She uses a quieter campaign approach.

One day, while Apple and her friends are in the town square, Mike Rophone introduces a brand-new candidate: Yolanda Yo-Yo.

Mike Rophone will host a debate between Apple and Yolanda in front of all of Shopville.

"Just smile if you get nervous," Lippy tells Apple. "It's all about confidence!"

Yolanda comes over to meet Apple and tell her a secret before the debate.
"I would never share it with anyone," Apple promises.
"I'm super nervous about the debate today," Yolanda admits.
"I'm nervous, too. But don't worry," Apple says. "The debate will be fun!"

Before the debate starts, a light falls from the stage!

Kooky swoops in to save the day.

"You're our hero!" says Lola Roller Blade.

Finally, the debate can begin. Mike Rophone asks, "Apple Blossom, why should we vote for you?"

"I have strong core values," Apple tells the crowd. "And I promise to lead with honesty!"

"But *I* know how to share my toys with my fellow Shopkins!" Yolanda cries. "Unlike Apple Blossom!"

She plays a tape recording of Apple's voice: "I would never share it with anyone."

The crowd gasps.

Yolanda's secret chat with Apple was all a trick! Apple tries to tell the crowd that the recording isn't what it sounds like. Will they still vote for Apple?

After the debate, Apple Blossom and Cheeky Chocolate hear voices in the toy store. It's Yolanda and Fortune Stella!

"When I become mayor, I'm going to pass this bill to make everyone in Shopville look and act just like me," Yolanda tells Stella, holding up a piece of paper. "Everyone will be a yo-yo!"

Apple and Cheeky hear every word. "I don't want to be a yo-yo!" says Cheeky.

"We have to grab that bill as evidence so no one votes for Yolanda!" Apple says.

But Yolanda is onto their plan and tears up her bill before they can get to it.

When Cheeky and Apple find their friends to share what they've heard, they discover a whole new problem. There's a new billboard in the town square. Yolanda put up a sign that says, "Bad Apple"!

"This has to end!" Apple cries, marching away to find Yolanda.

After Apple leaves, Kooky paints over Yolanda's mean message.

"What an honorable thing to do!" Freda Fern says.

Apple Blossom finds Yolanda by the fountain and challenges her to a Shop Quiz. Apple knows the answers to all of Mike Rophone's questions. Yolanda doesn't, but Fortune Stella helps her.

But then Stella says, "Ask again later," and Yolanda is stumped!

"Apple Blossom wins!" Mike announces.

It's time to vote. And it's a three-way tie between Apple, Yolanda, and Kooky!

"What do we do now?" asks Cheeky.

Kooky knows what to do. She pulls out the Shopville rule book.

"If there is a tie, a candidate can pass his or her votes to someone else," Kooky says. "I pass all of my votes to Apple Blossom."

Apple is the new mayor!

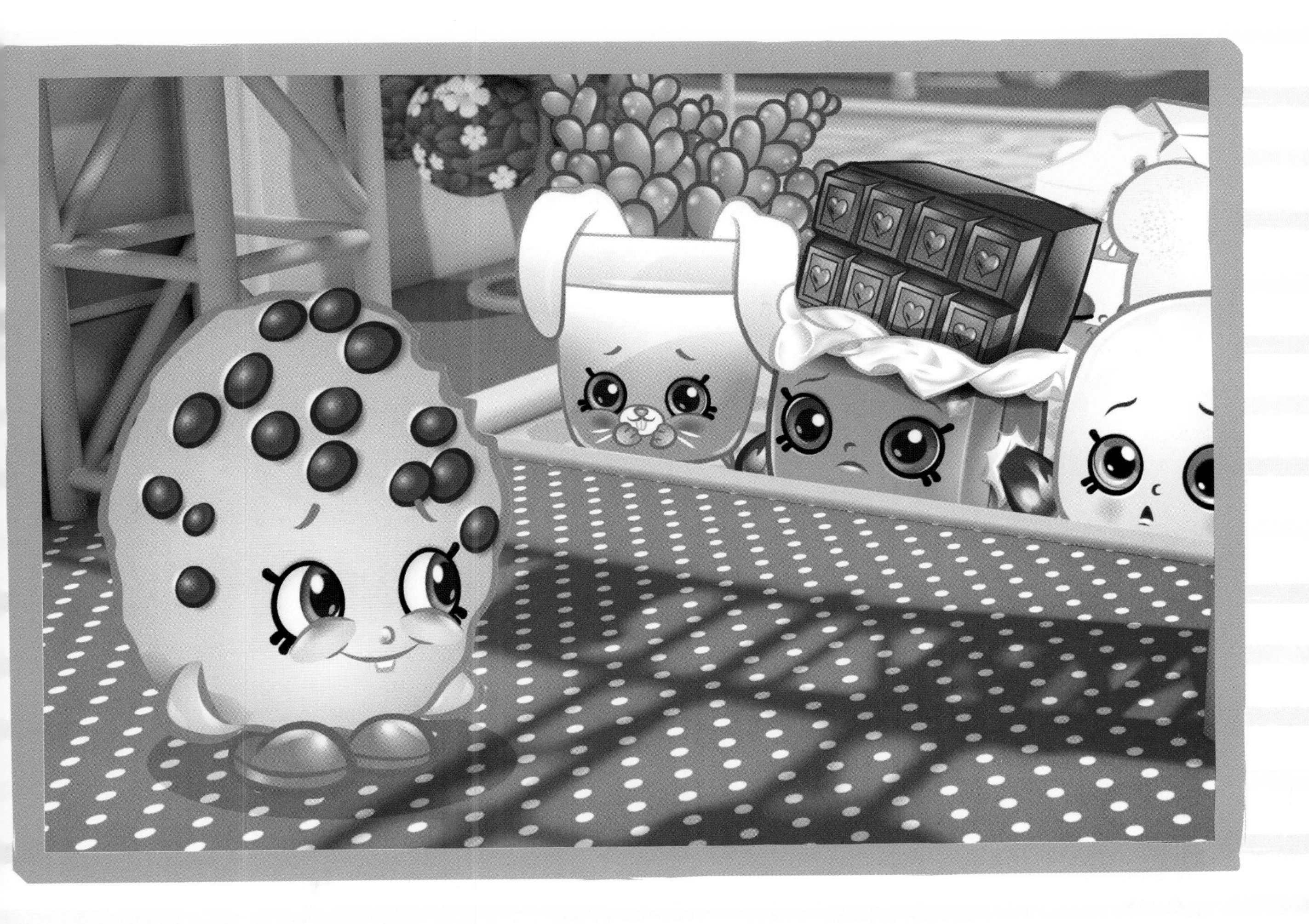

"I'm sorry you didn't win, Kooky," says Freda. "After you fixed all of Yolanda's mean signs about Apple!"

"Kooky, you did that for me?" Apple asks her friend.

Apple runs back onstage.

"Wait! While Yolanda and I have only been thinking about ourselves, Kooky has been helping everyone in Shopville. I pass all of my votes to her," she says.

Now Kooky is the mayor!

Yolanda starts to cry. "I feel so terrible. I just wanted to make everyone look like me so I would feel less self-conscious."

"It's okay to be different, Yolanda," Apple tells her. "That's what makes every Shopkin special!"

"I guess you're right!" Yolanda sniffles.

Now that Kooky is mayor, she wants to expand Shopville.
What will she build first?
Check ya later!

VOTE
KOOKY
I LOVE
SPK
AB
VOTE
#1
SPK
SPK
YO
YO
VOTE
S
SPK